For Natalee, Austin and Annika.
I love you and I love our hair.
H. L.

For Eva and Emma and their fantastic hair.
A. F.

FABER & FABER has published children's books since 1929. Some of our very first publications included *Old Possum's Book of Practical Cats* by T. S. Eliot starring the now world-famous Macavity, and *The Iron Man* by Ted Hughes. Our catalogue at the time said that 'it is by reading such books that children learn the difference between the shoddy and the genuine'. We still believe in the power of reading to transform children's lives.

First published in the UK in 2019
First published in the US in 2019
by Faber and Faber Limited
Bloomsbury House, 74–77 Great Russell Street, London WC1B 3DA
Text © Hannah Lee, 2019 Illustrations © Allen Fatimaharan, 2019
Designed by Faber and Faber
US HB ISBN 978–0–571–34686–8
PB ISBN 978–0–571–34687–5
All rights reserved.
Printed in India
10 9 8 7 6 5 4 3 2
The moral rights of Hannah Lee and Allen Fatimaharan have been asserted.
A CIP record for this book is available from the British Library.

FSC
www.fsc.org

MIX
Paper from
responsible sources
FSC® C016779

→ A FABER PICTURE BOOK ←

MY HAÏR

 Hannah Lee ✿ Allen Fatimarharan

90 YEARS OF EXCELLENCE

FABER & FABER

My birthday is coming up so soon,
I'll need new clothes to wear.

But most of all, I need to know,
How shall I style my hair?

"Let me do your hair," jokes Daddy.
"I'm getting better, I swear!"

Mommy rushes in the room,
"Daddy, don't you dare!"

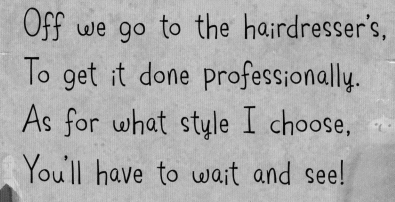

Off we go to the hairdresser's,
To get it done professionally.
As for what style I choose,
You'll have to wait and see!

Miss Dawn has lots of magazines,
Just so you can get a clue
Of the kind of hairstyle
That you would like to do!

Whilst I'm looking through them,
My imagination starts to grow,
I start to think of all the hairstyles
I already know!

Mommy has the most dazzling dreadlocks,
Such a joy to see them swing!
I like to practice braiding them,
It is my favorite thing!

My sister likes to experiment,
There's not a look that she won't try!

Bantu knots . . .

. . . a high top fade,

Braids, she's not shy!

My brothers both have cornrows,
With different shapes, patterns, and lines,
They love to show them off at school,
Yelling, "Come see the best designs!"

Daddy says, "Shave all over please!"
When he sits in the barber's chair.
His beard is shiny, curly, and full,
That's where he likes his hair!

Uncle has waves that are so smooth,
Swirling all over his head.
He keeps his hair brushed and neat
Don't forget the du-rag before bed!

Aunty's hair is shaved real short
Much like the head of a lioness!
She is so cool, stylish, and carefree,
That's how she likes it best!

Baby cousin is so small,
She hasn't much hair yet,
Already it's begun to grow,
She'll have loads soon, you can bet!

Grandma's hair is short and cropped,
There are many curls of grey,
She says she found one years ago
And invited them all to stay!

Grandpa wears turbans,

tie-heads, and scarves,

His hair tucked away from his face,
For Grandpa has so much hair,
That's how he keeps it in place!

Time to take a look at my friends,
And what styles they wear.
After all, I still don't know
How I'll style my hair!

Ryan will have braids with bows,
Her mommy can do them fast.
"Put a bonnet on," she says,
"To make the style last."

Michael has a mohawk,
Brandon a short back and sides.
They go to the barber's together,
And chat while the cutter glides!

Nina is my best friend,
"What style?" she asks with a pout.
"I want to try something new,
Maybe a twist out?"

"It's been forty-five minutes!" cries Miss Dawn,
"What will you do with your hair?
Time to let Mommy decide,
Don't you think that's fair?"

So Mommy whispers in my ear,
And that's exactly when I know,
The hairstyle that I will wear . . .

Will be my AFRO!

I love my Afro when it's out,
So BIG
and GREAT
and FREE.
My daddy says it is my crown,
It defies gravity!

A creation to which none
could compare,
I am so glad it is mine,

I love my hair!